Making Violet
A Sperm Donor Story

Erin DeVore

ISBN: 1546353828
ISBN-13: 978-1546353829

DEDICATION

For all the families created through the generosity and selflessness of donors and all the donors who have made families like ours whole.
For Violet, Desmond, and Gordon, for making my life whole.

Mommy and Violet were painting together on a bright sunny day.

Violet suddenly said, "All my purple has gone away!"

Mommy knew just what to do.

She mixed the red and the blue.

"This, my darling Violet, is like how we made you."

Violet loved this story!

Mommy loved to tell it:

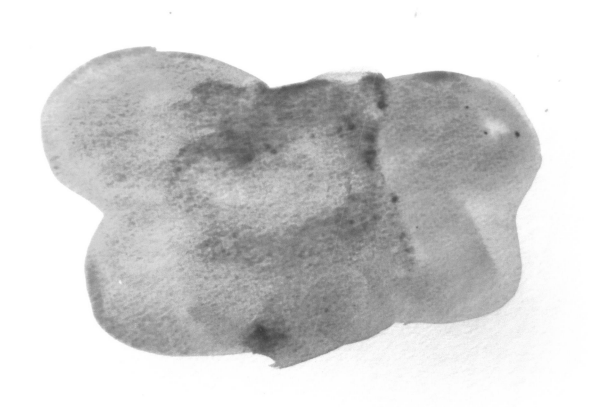

When Mommy and Daddy decided we wanted a baby, we knew we would need help. Making a baby is like making purple paint. You mix two things; sperm and an egg.

The egg comes from a woman, often the mommy.

The sperm comes from a man, often the daddy.

Not all families have a Mommy and a Daddy, and not all Mommies and Daddies can make healthy sperm and eggs, so there are helpers called donors who donate sperm or eggs to families who want to make a baby.

In our family, Mommy had healthy eggs, but Daddy couldn't make healthy sperm because of his Cystic Fibrosis.

We went to a doctor and then to a sperm bank to find a donor. The donor was anonymous, which means that we don't know who he is and he doesn't know who we are. We thank him for his gift of life, but he is not a part of our family.

It's like when you donate a coat or food to children in need- you don't get to pick who gets it or how they use it. You give without any expectations. You are a donor; someone who gives to those in need.

Some families choose a donor who is not anonymous, like someone they know and trust. That person may be a part of their family, or may just be a kind friend. Each family decides on their own how they'd like to build their family. It's a very personal choice, and we respect all the ways families are created.

Some families who need help making a baby choose to adopt a baby who needs a family, rather than create a new one.

Donor:
donates

Even though all babies begin with the same two ingredients, a sperm and an egg, they grow into all kinds of people with all kinds of families. Just like once you mix red and blue paint together, you could paint all different pictures. You can paint a sunset, a flower, a mermaid's tail, a mountain, a lion, a monster truck, or anything else you choose.

In so many ways, we are all the same, but we are also beautiful in our own ways too. And even though we are all made like the color purple, there's only one Violet just like you!

There's only one YOU too!

ABOUT THE AUTHOR

Erin is mom to two children born via sperm donor. She is a former public school teacher and now writes for her blogs KitchenGadgetVegan.com and WildflowerandBug.Weebly.com

When she was pregnant with Violet, her first baby, she couldn't find any children's books about being a child conceived via sperm/egg donor, and she believed in being open and honest with her children, so she wrote this book to help teach them and other children the beauty of how they were created.